BBFC·7

CR✓

Hurry!

ILLUSTRATED BY Emily Arnold McCully

adapted from *Farewell to the Farivox* by Harry Hartwick

Browndeer Press Harcourt, Inc. *San Diego   New York   London*

More than twenty years ago a story called Farewell to the Farivox, *by Harry Hartwick, was published for children. Although I came upon it many years after it was out of print, it immediately captured my imagination. This book is a way of saying thank you to the imaginative writer who created the farivox and who understood his poignant message.*

—E. A. M.

Original text copyright © 1972 by Harry Hartwick
Copyright © 2000 by Emily Arnold McCully

Requests for permission to make copies of any part of the work should be mailed to:
Permissions Department, Harcourt, Inc., 6277 Sea Harbor Drive,
Orlando, Florida 32887-6777.

Browndeer Press is a registered trademark of Harcourt, Inc.

Library of Congress Cataloging-in-Publication Data
McCully, Emily Arnold.
Hurry!/illustrated by Emily Arnold McCully,
adapted from *Farewell to the Farivox* by Harry Hartwick.
p. cm.
"Browndeer Press."
Summary: In 1916, a young boy living in Iowa named Tom Elson meets a
stranger who has an unusual animal called a farivox, maybe the last of its kind,
and Tom becomes determined to buy it.
[1. Wildlife conservation–Fiction.] I. Title.
PZ7.M478415Hu   2000
[Fic]–dc21   97-45564
ISBN 0-15-201579-5

First edition
A C E F D B

Printed in Hong Kong

The illustrations in this book were done
in watercolor on 140 lb. Arches paper.
The display type was hand lettered by Georgia Deaver.
The text type was set in Centaur.
Color separations by Bright Arts Ltd., Hong Kong
Printed by South China Printing Company, Ltd., Hong Kong
This book was printed on totally chlorine-free Nymolla Matte Art paper.
Production supervision by Stanley Redfern and Pascha Gerlinger
Designed by Lori McThomas Buley

For Jerry Berger

If you had been a boy or girl living on the American prairies in the early 1800s, you might have seen something no one will ever see again: the passenger pigeon. At that time there were so many of these birds that when they took to the air they actually darkened the sky. And when they settled in a wood to rest, their weight bent the branches almost to the ground, for often a single flock of pigeons contained millions of birds. No one dreamed they would ever become extinct. Yet they did. Hunters killed them by the thousands, and after a while there was only one lonely passenger pigeon left—in the Cincinnati Zoo. But it, too, died, in 1914—and then there was none.

And yet there *have* been instances when, long after people thought an animal was gone forever, one more turned up in some out-of-the-way place, much to the amazement of the person who found it. . . .

Perhaps the last person ever to see a farivox was a boy named Tom Elson, who lived in Vosburgh, Iowa, in the year 1916. At the time, he was ten years old and a student at McKinley Grade School there.

That particular Thursday in August began in a very ordinary way. At least, nothing happened to indicate that before the day was over Tom would have the most unusual experience of his whole life.

In the afternoon, after he washed the kitchen windows for his mother, Tom set off to the public library and returned some of the books he had had in his room.

As he left the library and came down Jackson Street, he passed the blacksmith shop and stopped to look into its dark, pungent depths. The shop smelled of hot iron and dust. All over the place were the blacksmith's tools, and there were hundreds of horseshoes, clinging to every surface like layers of strange, sleeping bats, wherever you looked. The blacksmith himself, Martin Krebs, nodded to Tom and smiled, without stopping his task of shaping a shoe on the anvil.

The horse waiting for the shoe, a gray mare, was standing beside the shafts of a wagon in front of the shop. Just inside the door, watching the smith, was the mare's owner, a fat man with pinched-up blue eyes. He was fanning himself with a straw hat.

A slight noise came from the bed of the wagon, and Tom went over to see what it was. It was a scratching sound, like chickens walking on tin. Peering over the side of the wagon, he saw a battered suitcase held together with rope. Up near the seat of the wagon was a rather large crate made of old boards roughly nailed together.

He went closer and leaned forward to look. The inside of the crate was dark, but there was something in there all right, something very odd-looking indeed. Tom couldn't believe his eyes. He blinked.

Its face was wide and flat, like a monkey's face, but it had a long body like a weasel's, with a bushy tail like that of a fox. Squinting his eyes at the floor of the crate, Tom could barely see the animal's small feet, which were clawed like a lion's. Its ears were tufted and sharp like those of a lynx, and it had a hooked beak like an owl's. From between the slats two yellow eyes stared out at him with a soft, burning light. Yet, for all their sharpness, there was something about the eyes that made Tom think the animal was actually smiling at him.

Tom looked at the fat man inside the doorway.

"Excuse me, sir," he said.

"Name's Murray Bayliss," replied the stranger. "At your service, my boy."

"Is that your animal in the crate?"

The other nodded.

"I've never seen anything like him! What's he called?"

"Why"—the fat man paused—"that's a farivox." He spelled it. "From the Latin: *fari* for speak, *vox* for voice. They're very rare now—you hardly ever see them."

"Where did you find this one?"

"Well, now, that's very strange. Usually they live further west, if any of them are left at all. How this one got into that cornfield near Warner City, I can't guess."

Tom peered inside the crate. It was pitch-black, but the yellow eyes of the farivox still gleamed at him. Suddenly he wanted the farivox very much.

The man continued. "It talks, you know."

"Talks!" echoed Tom in amazement. "Really *talks?*"

"None better," said the fat man, and Tom could see he was perfectly serious. "As well as you and I. You've heard of parrots talking, of course. Well, this animal, the farivox, talks better."

"Would you sell him, sir?" he asked.

"I might. For ten dollars," said the man rather sharply. "Or I'll keep him myself."

"Could he say something now?"

"I doubt that he would. He's shy with strangers."

"I see." Tom tried to remember how much money in coins he had in the cracked gravy boat his mother had given him to put on his dresser as a savings bank. It might even be that he had enough.

"Would you sell him to *me?*" he asked the stranger. "I'd take real good care of him."

The man looked down at him for a moment. "I might," he said again. "If you have the ten dollars—which I sort of doubt."

"I don't have it with me, but I can go home and get it," cried Tom, and he started off at once. "I'll be right back."

"Hurry," said the farivox.

Tom stopped. There was no doubt that the animal had spoken. It had said that one word clearly, just the way a human being would have said it, not gutturally, as you might expect an animal to speak, or croakingly, like a parrot.

"What did he say?" he asked the man.

The stranger looked a bit surprised. "I didn't hear anything," he said.

Tom looked at Mr. Krebs, who had been watching. But the blacksmith shook his head.

For a moment Tom hesitated. Then off he went for home, as fast as his legs would carry him.

He flew down the sidewalk in front of the house where the surly dog lived—the dog that tried to bite him every evening when he passed with his bag of newspapers—on past the house where a rooster once *had* bitten him as he tossed a paper on the porch. The surly dog barked madly as he went by, and the rooster took out after him. But Tom ran too fast for the rooster to catch him; he ran faster than he had ever run before, until he reached home.

He pounded onto the front porch, flung open the screen door, and dived inside. Up the stairs he went, to his room, two steps at a time, and grabbed the gravy boat on the dresser. It slipped from his hand, and the coins flew every which way. With a groan he started picking them up. Then, hands shaking, he began counting them. Nine dollars and eighty-one cents ... and eighty-two ... eighty-three.... That was all.

Then another thought. He leaped downstairs to the kitchen and hastily gathered up empty bottles he could return to the grocer. The grocery store was only a block away. He ran to it and flung open the door, causing the little bell that usually tinkled to jangle wildly. Tom dropped the bottles on the counter. It seemed to take the grocer forever to count them. Then he handed over the few coins. Ten dollars and two cents. It was enough!

In another few moments, Tom was back at the black-smith shop, half sick with breathlessness, but grinning triumphantly. And then slowly his grin turned to a look of horror. The wagon, the horse, the man, and the farivox were gone!

"He said he couldn't wait," explained Mr. Krebs, shaking hands with the handle of a small pump behind the forge and catching the cold water in a dented tin dipper. "Had to find a camping place before dark."

As Tom turned and walked away, tears stinging his eyes, it seemed to him that the light had died out of his life, as it was dying out of the late afternoon sky. When he reached home, he went upstairs and put the ten dollars and two cents back in the gravy boat on the dresser. Some-day he would buy something with it. But there was nothing that he would want as much as he had wanted the farivox.

As soon as school opened in the fall, he told his science teacher, Mr. Forbes, about the incident. The teacher wasn't sure, but he thought there had once been stories and legends about such an animal. The last one reported had been in San Francisco, where one was said to have been kept in a restaurant for the amusement of the diners. But after the earthquake there in 1906, there was no further word of it.

In the weeks that followed, Mr. Forbes and Tom sent letters all over the Middle West, trying to trace the man who called himself Murray Bayliss. But there was no money to pay for any real search, so in the end it was just as though the fat man, his gray horse, and the smiling farivox had all dried up and been blown away by the hot August wind, like dust on one of Iowa's long dirt roads.

Many of the natural wonders that our ancestors knew and loved still remain for us to enjoy. But many other things they took pleasure in have almost disappeared—like so many of our wild animals. Diseases have reduced their numbers. Streets, buildings, and highways have taken away their feeding grounds. And hunters have killed them. Many of the most beautiful and useful animals that once roamed America seem to have lost heart and faded away.

Yet here and there, in the wilder corners of our country, a few of these lost birds or beasts may still live on. And every now and then, someone walking over fields or exploring caves and rivers may see, for the last time, the only survivor of some long-vanished species . . .

. . . or hear the farivox say, *"Hurry."*